W9-BJO-598

Night House Bright House

Monica Wellington

DUTTON CHILDREN'S BOOKS • NEW YORK

For my parents and my sister, Laura,
and my daughter, Lydia

With special thanks to Andrew Kupfer, Barbara Lagow,
and Kelly Kynion, and always, Lucia Monfried

Reprinted by permission of
Dutton Children's Books, a
division of Penguin Books USA, Inc.

Library of Congress Cataloging-in-Publication Data
Wellington, Monica.
Night house, bright house/by Monica Wellington. — 1st ed.
p. cm.
Summary: During the night, all the objects in the house
wake up and cause an uproar.
[1. Night—Fiction. 2. Stories in rhyme.] 1. Title.
PZ8.3.W4595Ni 1997 [E]—dc20 96-24550 CIP AC

Published in the United States 1997 by Dutton Children's Books,
a division of Penguin Books USA Inc.
375 Hudson Street, New York, New York 10014
Designed by Amy Berniker and Sara Reynolds
Printed in USA
First Edition
2 4 6 8 10 9 7 5 3 1

Gouache, watercolors, and colored pencils were
used to create the full-color art for this book.

"Time to get up,"

said the cup.

Waking, Shaking in the Studio

"Shh—it's night," said the  light.

"Pit-a-pat," said the  mat.

"Chug-chug," said the  jug.

"Jingle-jangle," said the 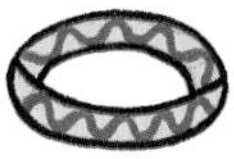 bangle.

"Clinkety-clank," said the  bank.

"Loop-de-loop," said the 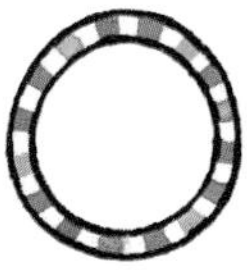 hoop.

"You're bad," said the  pad.

"GO," said the  bow.

ABCDEF
GHIJKL
MNOPQ
RSTUVW
XYZ
Lydia
DON'T DISTURB
I Lo
Cat
Mice

Sneaking, Peeking in the Bedroom

"What's that noise?" said the toys.

"Quiet down," said the crown.

"We need to sleep," said the sheep.

"Yakety-yak," said the sack.

"Gobbledygook," said the book.

"Doodle-de-doo," said the shoe.

"What an uproar," said the door.

"Move on," said the swan.

Helter, Skelter
Down the Stairs

"Here they come," said the drum.

"Higgledy-pop," said the mop.

"Dickory-dock," said the clock.

"Fiddle-dee-dee," said the key.

"Ziggity-zag," said the bag.

"Scoot," said the boot.

"Scat," said the hat.

"Now scram," said the pram.

Maple Syrup
HONEY
COFFEE
Peanut Butter
FLOUR
Rice
TEA
S
P
SUGAR
Catsup
mustard
Butter
Mice Times

Racing, Chasing to the Kitchen

"Get ready," said the  spaghetti.

"Here they are," said the  jar.

"What a clutter," said the butter.

"Don't get flustered," said the 

mustard.

"Look out, please," said the cheese.

"Tickle-tickle," said the 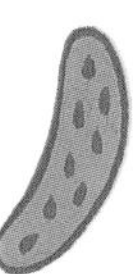 pickle.

"Phony-baloney," said the macaroni.

"Run," said the bun.

SOAP
H
C
H
C

Dashing, Splashing in the Bathroom

"Rub-a-dub," said the tub.

"Drippity-drip," said the ship.

"What a mess," said the dress.

"They'll clean up," said the cup.

"You think?" said the sink.

"Let's hope," said the soap.

"Fat chance," said the pants.

"Lots of luck," said the duck.

Giggling, Wiggling in the Living Room

"Crash, boom!" said the  broom.

"Oh NO," said the  domino.

"Don't look," said the  book.

"I'm fainting," said the  painting.

"Did something break?" said the 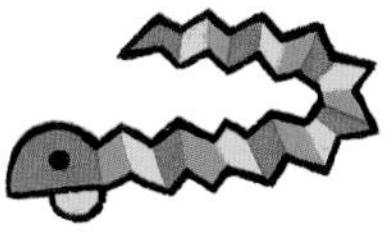 snake.

"You bet," said the TV  set.

"Boo-hoo," said the  statue.

"Spells trouble," said the 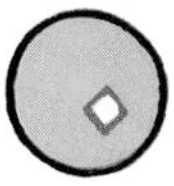 bubble.

Telephone Book
Yellow Pages
A
B
C

Twirling, Whirling in the Front Hall

"Slow down," said the clown.

"For my sake," said the cake.

"How exhausting," said the frosting.

"Just crazy," said the daisy.

"Super-silly," said the lily.

"Leave things alone," said the phone.

"You're telling me," said the key.

"Stay cool," said the jewel.

Bumping, Jumping in the Dining Room

"Surprise!" said the  pies.

"This is great," said the 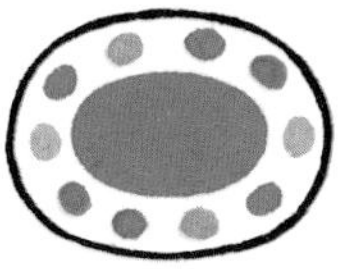 plate.

"First-class," said the  glass.

"Just dandy," said the  candy.

"A dream," said the  ice cream.

"I'm tired out," said the  spout.

"I agree," said the  tea.

"Enough's enough," said the  cream puff.

I Love You
INK
2
1 3

Pattering, Clattering in the Back Hall

"Just stop," said the  top.

"It's late," said the  skate.

"I suppose," said the  rose.

"Poppycock," said the  block.

"We're done in," said the  pin.

"Get upstairs," said the  bears.

"It's about time," said the  chime.

"That's what I think," said the  ink.

JUNE
M T W Th F S Su
1 2 3 4 5
6 7 8 9 10 11 12
13 14 15 16 17 18 19
20 21 22 23 24 25 26
27 28 29 30
ABCDEF
GHIJKL
MNOPQ
RSTUVW
XYZ
Happy Birthday
MICE
rice
dice
nice
CAT
mat
fat
rat
Night House
AK
I LOVE YOU

Back in the Bedroom, Snuggling, Cuddling

"Hush," said the  brush.

"Pipe down," said the  crown.

"Curl up," said the  cup.

"Snug as a bug," said the  rug.

"Close your eyes," said the  ties.

"Sweet dreams, mice," said the  dice.

"Sleep tight," said the  kite.

"Love you," said the  shoe.

"That's all,"

said the ball.